By Lynn Hodges & Sue Buchanan

A Song of God's Love

Illustrated by John Bendall Brunello

I Love You THIS Much

Zonderkidz

To our "Little Foursome"—Lexie, Ellie, Allie, and Mary Peyton.
We love you *more* than this much.
—L.H. and S.B.

For my darling wife, Tiziana,
and Billy (our cat).
—J.B.B.

Zonder**kidz**™

The children's group of Zondervan

I Love You This Much
ISBN: 0-310-23268-6
Copyright © 2001 by Lynn Hodges and Sue Buchanan
Illustrations copyright © 2001 by John Bendall Brunello
Words © 2000 by Lynn Hodges and Sue Buchanan
Music © 2000 by Lynn Hodges
Performance ℗ 2000 by Lynn Hodges and Mary Peyton

Requests for information should be addressed to:
Zonderkidz, Grand Rapids, Michigan 49530

Published in association with the literary agency of Alive Communications, Inc., 7680 Goddard St., Suite 200, Colorado Springs, CO 80920.

Design by Chris Tobias
Art direction by Jody Langley

Printed in China
02 03 04 05 /HK/ 4

I pray that you ... may have power ...
to grasp how wide and long and high
and deep is the love of Christ.

Ephesians 3:17-18 (NIV)

When you arise with sleepy eyes,
my smiling face you see.

I always say, "Well, look who's up."
You laugh and say, "It's me!"

How I love your morning hug;
you nestle in my touch.
You wait to hear me whisper low,
"I LOVE YOU THIS MUCH."

I love you best.
I love you most.

I love you high.
I love you low.

I love you deep.
I love you wide.

I LOVE YOU
THIS MUCH!

Throughout the day,
we hide and seek;

I love to see you smile.

I always say,
"I found you, dear"

But I had you all
the while.

You run to me
with open arms;

I love to feel
your touch.

We shout out loud for all to hear,

"I LOVE YOU
THIS MUCH!"

I love you best.

I love you most.

I love you high.

I love you low.

I love you deep.

I love you wide.

I LOVE YOU THIS MUCH!

I trust you know that God is so,
by what I say and do.

I tell you he is safe and sure.

And what he says is true.

He holds you in his loving arms;
you feel his tender touch.

You hear the heavenly Father say,
"I love you this much!"

When day is done at setting sun,
we bow our heads and pray.

I trust you to God's loving care.

You safely drift away.

I kiss you on
your sleepy head,
with one last
gentle touch.

The words still ringing in our ears,
"I LOVE YOU THIS MUCH."

I love you best. I love you most.
I love you high. I love you low.
I love you deep. I love you wide.
I love you, I love you,
I LOVE YOU THIS MUCH!